I Will Love You Forever

A very long time ago

a mother Maiasaura found a tiny egg in the forest after a storm.

"Poor thing. If that nasty Tyrannosaurus finds it, he will eat it."

The kind mother Maiasaura took the egg back to her home.

TATSUYA MIYANISHI
MUSEYON, New York

Tenderly she held her
own egg and the egg
that she'd found.

"Hatch soon and
be healthy,"
she whispered.

The mother Maiasaura held the eggs close every day.

Many days went by. . . .

One day the mother Maiasaura came home after gathering red berries.

CRICK CRACK

The babies were hatching!

The baby that came out of the egg from the forest was a Tyrannosaurus.

The mother Maiasaura was worried.

When the baby finds out that he's a Tyrannosaurus, it will be a disaster.

That night she took the sleeping baby Tyrannosaurus in her arms and quietly left home.

She reached the place in the forest where she had found the egg and, with an aching heart, placed the sleeping baby on the ground.

She turned toward home.

Then she heard, "Kooo . . ."

The baby was calling her!

Holding the baby tightly in her arms, she returned home.

It was a quiet, starry night.

The mother Maiasaura thought carefully about the babies' names.

"You are always happy and cheerful. Your name is Light," she said to the baby Maiasaura.

"You are strong and powerful, but I would like you to be kind. Your name is Heart," she said to the baby Tyrannosaurus.

Light and Heart ate red berries and grew quickly.

They were close and got on well—just like brothers.

One day Light met an Ankylosaurus.

"Watch where you are going, little one. You'll be in big trouble if a Tyrannosaurus sees you alone."

"What is a Tyrannosaurus?" Light asked.

"Tyrannosaurs are nasty, violent bullies. No one likes them. They have sharp claws and jagged fangs, and their bodies are rough all over."

Light returned home and said, "Mom, Mister Ankylosaurus taught me about the scary Tyrannosaurs. Their claws are sharp, their fangs are jagged, and their bodies are rough. . . . That sounds just like Heart, doesn't it?"

His mother got angry.

"Stop it, Light! Heart is your brother! Never talk like that again!"
The mother Maiasaura hugged her two boys tightly.

"I . . . I'm sorry, Heart," mumbled Light.

The days turned into months.

Light and Heart grew as tall as their mother.

It was Heart's job to get red berries for the family.

One day he was out looking
for berries when suddenly from
behind a rocky mountain . . .

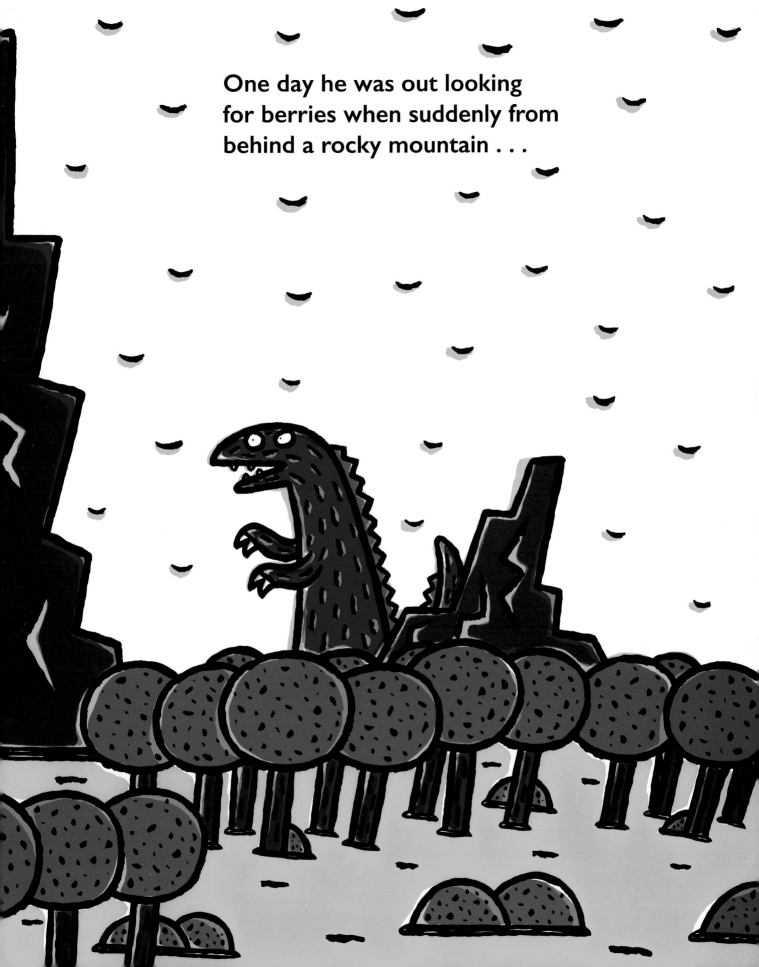

ROAR!

A Tyrannosaurus with blazing eyes jumped out at Heart.

But when he saw Heart, the Tyrannosaurus was disappointed.

I thought I smelled a yummy Maiasaura, but this is a Tyrannosaurus like me.

Heart looked at the Tyrannosaurus and thought,

The sharp claws, jagged fangs, and rough body . . . this could be a Tyrannosaurus . . . .

"M-mister, what are you?" Heart asked nervously.

"Are you talking to me? Can't you see
I'm the same as you?"
the Tyrannosaurus replied.

Heart was relieved.

*He isn't a Tyrannosaurus.
He's a Maiasaura
like me, he thought. Whew!*

"What are you doing out here?"
the Tyrannosaurus asked.

Heart smiled.

"I am on my way to get some delicious food,"
he answered, imagining lots of red berries.

"Is that so? I'm also on my way to get some delicious food."

The Tyrannosaurus was imagining lots of Maiasauras.

Oh, okay! He's also going to gather red berries, Heart thought.

"Today I'll fill your stomach. Just follow me.
He, he, he . . ."

Heart followed the Tyrannosaurus.

As they walked by the forest,
the Tyrannosaurus stopped and said sadly,

"Long ago, during a storm, I lost my precious egg in this forest."

Heart wasn't paying attention.

"Hey, look," he said "There are tons of red berries here. Why don't we pick them?"

"We don't eat that kind of thing," replied the Tyrannosaurus, "There are some delicious Maiasauras waiting just on the other side of the forest. He, he . . ."

"M-mister, aren't red berries the delicious food you were thinking of?" Heart asked. "M-mister, are you a Tyrannosaurus?"

"Of course I am a Tyrannosaurus! I said that we're the same. And you're a Tyrannosaurus."

"No. . . . I-I'm a Maiasaura!"

"Don't be foolish, kid. Look at your sharp claws, jagged fangs, and rough body. You are definitely a Tyrannosaurus."

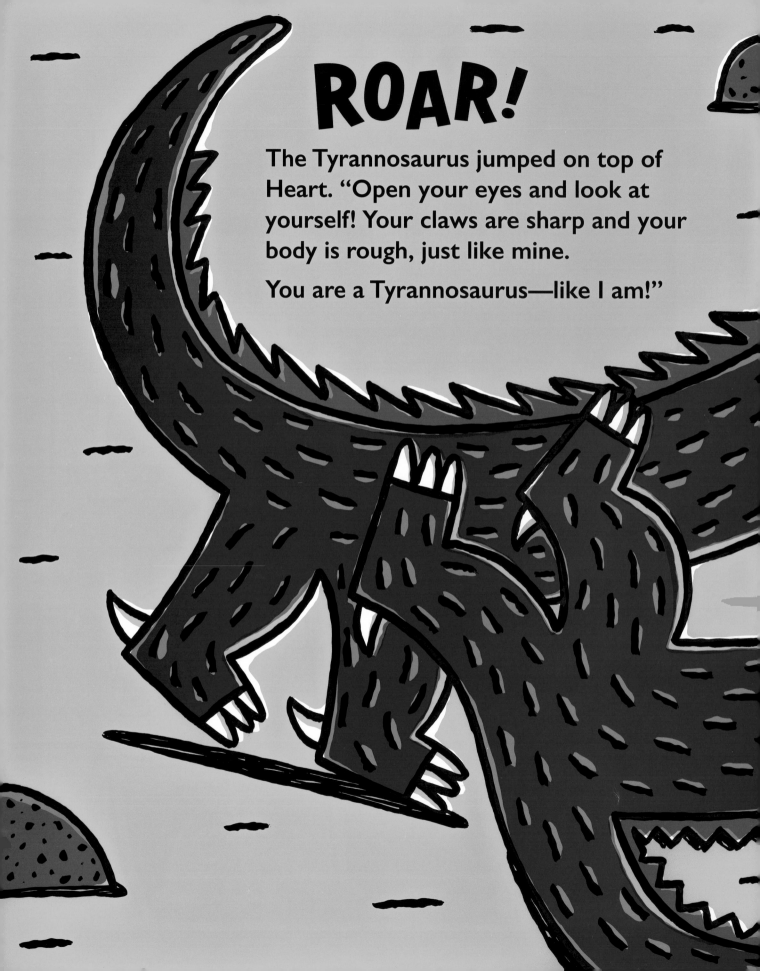

ROAR!

The Tyrannosaurus jumped on top of Heart. "Open your eyes and look at yourself! Your claws are sharp and your body is rough, just like mine.

You are a Tyrannosaurus—like I am!"

The Tyrannosaurus's arms
were next to Heart's.
His skin was rough;
his claws were sharp.
They looked exactly
the same as Heart's.
Heart closed his eyes.

"I can't be. . . .
I'm not . . ."

AAAARGH!

His mother heard him crying.

"Heart is coming back, and he's upset. What happened?"

Heart's mother held him close.

With tears in his eyes, Heart asked,

"Mom, am I . . . am I a Tyrannosaurus? Am I your child?"

His mother hugged Heart as tight as she could.

"You are my dear child, Heart. You are my treasure."

"Thank you, Mom," Heart said, tears rolling down his cheeks. "I'm Heart, aren't I?"

Heart turned around and saw the Tyrannosaurus approaching, his eyes blazing.

Heart ran.

"Where are you going?"
his mother shouted.

Heart looked at her and smiled.

"I'm going to gather red berries.
I'll be back with lots of them."

Then Heart roared and charged
toward the
Tyrannosaurus.

The Tyrannosaurus didn't fight back. Tears fell from his eyes too.

Heart looked at the Tyrannosaurus and stopped biting.

Could this be my . . ., he wondered.

Heart never came back.

One day the mother Maiasaura found a large pile of red berries in the place where she had found Heart.

"Oh, my dear Heart, . . . wherever you are, I will love you forever. Always and forever."

Then she put a red berry into her mouth.

I WILL LOVE YOU FOREVER

Anata wo Zutto Zutto Aishiteru © 2006 Tatsuya Miyanishi
All rights reserved.

Translation by Mariko Shii Gharbi
English editing by Simone Kaplan

Library of Congress Cataloging-in-Publication Data

Names: Miyanishi, Tatsuya, 1956- author, illustrator. | Gharbi, Marido Shii, translator. | Kaplan, Simone, editor.
Title: I will love you forever / Tatsuya Miyanishi ; translation by Mariko Shii Gharbi ; English editing by
    Simone Kaplan.
Other titles: Anata wo zutto zutto aishiteru. English
Description: New York : Museyon, [2017] | Series: Tyrannosaurus series ; book 4 | "Originally published in Japan
    in 2006 by POPLAR Publishing Co., Ltd."--Title page verso. | Summary: A female Maiasaura finds a lost egg
    in the forest and decides to look after it with her own egg. Surprisingly, a baby tyrannosaurus hatches from
    the egg! The greathearted mother accepts and raises him as her own son, Heart. One day, Heart goes to
    pick berries and comes across another tyrannosaurus. Heart then makes a tough decision and leaves his
    family behind to discover who he really is. The fourth title in this series, 'I Will Love You Forever' delivers a
    heart warming story about adoption with vivid illustrations and endearlingly drawn characters.--Publisher.
Identifiers: ISBN: 978-1-940842-17-2 | LCCN: 2016963313
Subjects: LCSH: Tyrannosaurus rex--Juvenile fiction. | Maiasaura--Juvenile fiction. |
    Dinosaurs--Juvenile fiction. | Mother and child--Juvenile fiction. | Love--Juvenile fiction. |
    Adoption--Juvenile fiction. | CYAC: Tyrannosaurus rex--Fiction. | Maiasaura--Fiction. |
    Disosaurs--Fiction. | Mother and child--Fiction. | Love--Fiction. | Adoption--Fiction. | BISAC:
    JUVENILE FICTION / Animals / Dinosaurs & Prehistoric Creatures.
Classification: LCC: PZ7.M699575 I184 2017 | DDC: [E]--dc23

Published in the United States and Canada by:
Museyon Inc.
1177 Avenue of the Americas, 5th Floor
New York, NY 10036

Museyon is a registered trademark.
Visit us online at www.museyon.com

Originally published in Japan in 2006 by POPLAR Publishing Co., Ltd.
English translation rights arranged with POPLAR Publishing Co., Ltd.

Printed in China

ISBN 9781940842172